MISSION ALERT

ISLAND X

Darby Creek
A division of Lerner Publishing Group, Inc.
241 First Avenue North
Minneapolis, MN 55401 USA

For reading levels and more information, look up this title at
www.lernerbooks.com.

Main body text set in ITC Goudy Sans Std 14/24.
Typeface provided by Monotype Typography.

Library of Congress Cataloging-in-Publication Data

Names: Hulme-Cross, Benjamin, author. | Damerum, Kanako,
illustrator. | Takasaki, Yuzuru, illustrator.
Title: Island X / Benjamin Hulme-Cross ; illustrated by Kanako and Yuzuru.
Description: Minneapolis, MN : Darby Creek, [2018] | Series: Mission alert | "First published
in 2017 by Bloomsbury Education." | Summary: "Tom and Zilla are regular boarding school
students—except when they're working as special agents for the government. Their next
mission is to investigate the private island of a shady millionaire"— Provided by publisher.
Identifiers: LCCN 2018007209 (print) | LCCN 2018014493 (ebook) | ISBN 9781541525894
(eb pdf) | ISBN 9781541525795 (lb : alk. paper) | ISBN 9781541526334 (pb :
alk. paper) | ISBN 9781472929570 (ePub) | ISBN 9781472929587 (ePDF)
Subjects: | CYAC: Spies—Fiction. | Brothers and sisters—Fiction. |
Twins—Fiction. | Wealth—Fiction. | Islands—Fiction.
Classification: LCC PZ7.1.H86 (ebook) | LCC PZ7.1.H86 Isl 2018 (print) | DDC [Fic]—dc23

LC record available at https://lccn.loc.gov/2018007209

Manufactured in the United States of America
1-44563-35494-4/4/2018

MISSION ALERT
ISLAND X

BENJAMIN HULME-CROSS

Illustrated by
Kanako and Yuzuru

MINNEAPOLIS

Tom and his twin sister Zilla go to a boarding
school. They don't like it very much. But
Tom and Zilla have a secret. They work as
spies for the Secret Service. Sometimes there
is a spy mission that children are better at
than grown-ups. That's when Tom and Zilla
get their next Mission Alert!

CONTENTS

Chapter One

Zilla and Tom were playing soccer with some friends. Suddenly Zilla stopped running. Her watch was buzzing. She looked over at Tom.

She could tell that his watch was buzzing too. That could mean only one thing. The Secret Service had a new mission for them!

Zilla pretended that she had hurt her leg. Tom ran over to help Zilla off the field.

They sat down under a tree where no one could see them, and then they plugged earphones into their watches.

The watches had lots of special spy features. The Secret Service could find Zilla and Tom at any time by tracking their watches.

They tapped the screens and the instructions began.

"Agents, here is your next mission," they heard Marcus say. Marcus was their handler at Mission Control.

"There is a company called Starcorp," he said.

"They make satellites and lots of other high tech stuff. The owner of Starcorp is the billionaire Boris Silver," Marcus explained.

Tom and Zilla knew the name Silver. There was a boy in their class called Jake Silver. Boris Silver was his dad.

Tom and Zilla didn't like Jake.

Not many people did. He was the sort of kid who showed off because his dad was rich.

"Boris Silver owns an island," said Marcus.

Everyone at school knew that Jake Silver's dad owned an island. Jake was always bragging about it.

"We have been spying on Boris Silver," said Marcus, "He has built a second island next to the first."

Jake and Zilla saw some pictures on their watch screens.

They were photos of the islands, taken from the sky.

"We are calling this new island Island X," explained Marcus.

"Look closely at the round building on Island X. Silver says that this is where he is developing a super-powerful telescope."

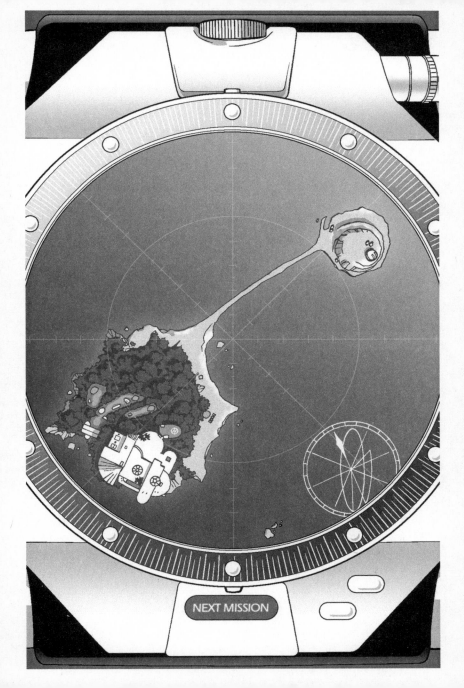

NEXT MISSION

Tom and Zilla saw more pictures on their watch screens. One picture showed a round building with an area of the roof pulled back.

"The Secret Service is worried," explained Marcus, "because when our satellites fly over the islands we lose contact with them."

"So you think that Silver is using his telescope to jam the signal from our satellites?" asked Tom.

"But why would he do that?" said Zilla.

"Boris Silver makes and sells satellites," said Marcus. "But the government has never bought any of his satellites. We don't trust him. We think he is trying to stop our satellites from working properly so that we will be forced to buy his. It's all about money."

"OK. So you want us to find out what is happening on Island X," said Zilla.

"That's right," said Marcus. "Good luck!"

Chapter Two

Zilla and Tom had a plan. They decided they would pretend to be best friends with Jake Silver. Then he would invite them to visit his dad's island.

They sat next to him at dinner. They cheered him on at soccer. They even laughed at his jokes. Jake wasn't used to having any friends because he showed off so much. He was so happy that he invited Zilla and Tom to visit his dad's island.

So over spring break Zilla, Tom, and Jake went to Boris Silver's island. They flew in Boris Silver's private helicopter. As they were about to land they looked down and saw Island X for the first time.

"See?" shouted Jake. "I told you this would be amazing. I bet you've never done anything this cool!"

Tom and Zilla looked at each other. Jake was showing off again, but they didn't say anything.

The helicopter landed, and Jake led Tom and Zilla toward a very grand house. A huge man wearing fancy clothes opened the door. He stared hard at Tom and Zilla.

"Get out of our way," Jake shouted rudely at the man. "I'll show Tom and Zilla around the house. You get our bags from the helicopter!"

The man looked very annoyed at being told what to do by a boy, but he just said, "Very good, sir."

"That's Simpson, our butler," said Jake. "He has to do what I tell him."

Tom and Zilla looked at each other, but they didn't say anything.

"Hey, Jake, can we explore the island first?" Tom asked. "This place is epic!"

"Okay," said Jake. He was pleased that Tom and Zilla thought his dad's island was amazing.

As they set off to explore the island, they saw the helicopter taking off. Simpson was looking up at it and shouting into a walkie-talkie.

The island was quite small, and it only took them about half an hour to walk around it.

When they came to the point where they could see Island X, Tom began asking questions. Jake told them that his dad had built Island X as a place where Starcorp could test telescopes.

"But why did he need to build a whole island?" Tom wanted to know. "Why not just buy a field or something?"

"Oh, stop asking so many questions!" Jake said crossly. "If my dad wants to build an island, he builds an island. And I'm going to be just like him when I grow up."

Zilla looked across at Island X. She could see one side of the round building. And on top of the wall she could see guards.

It looked like they were holding weapons.

Zilla saw that the guards were pointing

those weapons at her . . .

Chapter Three

Jake's room was full of very expensive things.

There were game consoles. There was a huge TV.

There was even a drone in one corner of the room.

"You've got to see this game," Jake said, giving them both handsets. "My dad bought it for me and it's not even out yet. Nobody else has it."

They sat down on giant bean bags and began playing Jake's new game. The rest of the day was the same. Jake kept bragging about his amazing life.

He was rude to Simpson the butler. He bossed Tom and Zilla around. Tom and Zilla let him win the new game. They were getting really fed up when the door to Jake's room burst open.

"Dad!" said Jake. He didn't sound happy. He sounded scared.

Boris Silver did not even look at Jake.

He stared at Tom and then Zilla. "Who are you?" he asked sternly.

"These are my friends I told you about . . ." Jake began.

"Shut up!" Boris shouted. "You don't have friends because nobody likes you."

He turned to Zilla. "Why are you really here?" he asked.

Zilla felt really scared, but she also felt angry. Why was Boris Silver so horrible to Jake?

"How can you talk to your own son like that?" Zilla said. "We're here because we *are* Jake's friends. And if you don't want him making friends then don't send him to school!"

Boris stared at Zilla. He looked so angry. But then he turned around and walked out of the room.

"Phew!" said Zilla.

"Is he always like that?" Tom asked.

"Not always," said Jake. He sounded a bit like he might cry. "He's only that angry when something important is going on with his work . . ."

Chapter Four

Later that night, when everyone was in bed, Zilla's watch began flashing. This was the signal she and Tom had picked. Time to check out Island X!

She quietly got out of bed, put her clothes on, and tiptoed out into the hallway to meet Tom.

They crept downstairs. Every time a floorboard creaked they stopped to listen in case anyone had heard them. Tom led the way toward the large front door.

He was about ten steps away from it when he stopped and held his hand up. Zilla nearly bumped into his back. Suddenly, she saw why he had stopped. Sitting in a chair near the front door was Simpson the butler!

They stayed quite still, waiting for him to jump up and shout at them.

Then they heard a noise. It was the sound of snoring. Simpson was asleep.

They crept on. The door opened with a soft click. Simpson kept snoring as Tom and Zilla went outside.

"Now for the hard part!" Zilla whispered.

But she was wrong. Everything went smoothly. They walked over to Island X without any problems.

They could see the outline of the round building.

Zilla stared at the top of the wall, but she couldn't see any guards up there. They heard a noise coming from behind them. They stopped and listened, but they heard nothing else.

They began creeping around the edge of the building. At last they came to a small door.

Zilla tapped at her watch and clicked on the lock-pick app. She held the watch against the door where she guessed the lock would be.

The app undid the lock, and they heard it click open. Zilla turned the handle and pushed the door open. They both stepped inside.

They were standing on a metal walkway, high up on the side of a large room. The room was huge. It went down deep into the ground.

There were about twenty men and women in white coats at computers around the edge of the room. It was like the inside of a factory. In the middle was a huge machine with a barrel that pointed straight up.

There was a grinding noise. Zilla grabbed Tom's arm and pointed up.

The roof above the machine was slowly opening. Zilla switched her phone to camera mode and began filming.

"It looks like they're about to use it, whatever it is," said Tom.

"British satellite M-I-S 523 coming into range in five minutes!" one of the men called out.

"Ready to send jamming signal!" said another.

"So they *are* trying to mess up the satellites!" Zilla whispered. "Marcus should be getting live video from my watch. The army will be here in a few minutes."

And then they each felt a large hand on their shoulder.

"Gotcha!" said Simpson.

Chapter Five

Simpson led Tom and Zilla down to the huge machine. Boris Silver was standing there. He had a nasty smile on his face.

"I *knew* you were here to cause trouble!" said Boris Silver. "Of course, I won't be able to let you go now. You've seen too much."

"Did you really think there weren't any guards on duty tonight? I knew you wanted to see inside these secret buildings, and I wanted to catch you in the act!" Silver laughed.

"And what did you catch us doing?" Zilla asked. "We were just having a look around."

"YOU ARE SPIES!" Silver shouted. "But you are *not* going to stop me. I am going to see to it that every object in space is owned by Starcorp. And two kids are not going to get in my way!"

"That's where you're wrong," said Tom. "We've been recording everything you've been saying."

Zilla held up her watch.

Boris Silver looked so angry Tom thought he might burst.

Suddenly, there was a shout and the sound of lots of boots on the metal staircase. The soldiers Zilla had called had arrived.

* * *

A short while later Tom and Zilla stood on the lawn outside the main house. Jake was with them. The soldiers had woken him up. Two men led Boris Silver across the lawn toward an army helicopter. He was in handcuffs, and he shouted at the soldiers all the way to the helicopter.

"Sorry about your dad, Jake," said Tom.

"It's Okay," said Jake quietly. "Home is going to be a better place without him around."

Guess Who?

Each of the quotes below comes from one of these characters in the story:

1. Zilla
2. Tom
3. Marcus
4. Jake
5. Boris

Match the character to the quote by writing down the correct letter next to the character's number. Check your answers at the end of this section.

a. "Oh, stop asking so many questions!"

b. "It looks like they're about to use it, whatever it is."

c. "You don't have friends because nobody likes you."

d. "Agents, here is your next mission."

e. "How can you talk to your own son like that?"

Great Gadget!

Zilla and Tom have some very cool watches. Look at the list of watch features below and write down the letters of the ones that are used during their Island X mission:

a. They buzz to alert the children to a new mission.

b. You can plug earphones into them.

c. You can send an email from them.

d. They have a tracking device built in.

e. You can watch a movie on them when flying on a plane.

f. They can display photos of important places that are part of the mission before Tom and Zilla go on the mission.

g. They change color.

h. They contain a lock-pick app.

i. They can film things the children see.

j. They show the temperature in a building.

What Next?

- Would you like to do secret missions like Zilla and Tom? Why or why not?
- Even though Jake's dad has lots of money and Jake has lots of things, he is not happy. What does Jake want his dad to do differently?
- Do you think Zilla and Tom will still be friends with Jake after the mission? Give reasons for your answer based on events in the story.
- Design your own gadget that could be used on a spy mission. Think about what features it would need to have and how these could be hidden from enemies. Draw a picture of your design and add labels to show all the features.

Answers to Guess Who?

1e, 2b, 3d, 4a, 5c

Answers to Great Gadget!

a, b, d, f, h, i

MISSION ALERT

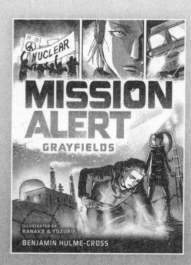

MISSION ALERT
GRAYFIELDS

ILLUSTRATED BY
KANAKO & YUZURU

BENJAMIN HULME-CROSS

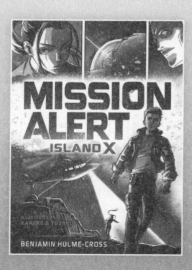

MISSION ALERT
ISLAND X

ILLUSTRATED BY
KANAKO & YUZURU

BENJAMIN HULME-CROSS

Look out for Tom and Zilla's
next spy mission!

CHECK OUT ALL THE TITLES IN THE
MISSION ALERT SERIES

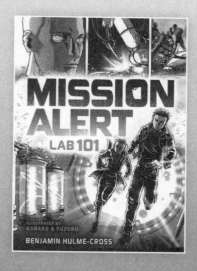

LEVEL UP

WHAT WOULD YOU DO IF YOU WOKE UP IN A VIDEO GAME?

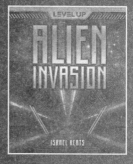

ALIEN INVASION
ISRAEL KEATS

LABYRINTH
ISRAEL KEATS

POD RACER
R.T. MARTIN

REALM OF MYSTICS
RAELYN DRAKE

SAFE ZONE
R.T. MARTIN

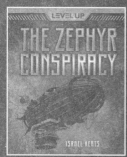

THE ZEPHYR CONSPIRACY
ISRAEL KEATS

CHECK OUT ALL THE TITLES IN THE
LEVEL UP SERIES

MASON FALLS MYSTERIES

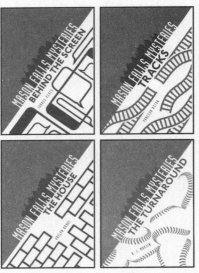

EVEN AN ORDINARY TOWN HAS ITS SECRETS.

ATTACK ◆ ON EARTH

WHEN ALIENS INVADE,
ALL YOU CAN DO IS SURVIVE.

DESERTED

THE FALLOUT

THE FIELD TRIP

GETTING HOME

LOCKDOWN

TAKE SHELTER

CHECK OUT ALL THE TITLES IN THE
ATTACK ON EARTH SERIES

About the Author

Benjamin Hulme-Cross has written over thirty books for emerging young readers. Prior to becoming a full-time writer, he worked for a publishing company, editing novels and plays for high schools. He is currently the director for Iffley Publishing in the United Kingdom.

About the Illustrators

Kanako and Yuzuru are two Japanese sisters who collaborate on every illustration, even though Kanako lives in London and Yuzuru resides in Japan. Using traditional pen and ink, plus a computer, they have done many illustration projects for children's publishing.